Graphic design and illustrations: Zapp
Story adaptation: Jane Brierley

© 1996 Tormont Publications Inc.
  338 Saint Antoine St. East
  Montreal, Canada H2Y 1A3
  Tel. (514) 954-1441
  Fax (514) 954-5086

THE EMPEROR'S NEW CLOTHES

TORMONT

There was once a very grand emperor who loved fine clothes. He spent almost all his time and a great deal of money on splendid new outfits.

The emperor wasn't very interested in governing his country, and only appeared in public to show off some new fashion.

One day, two swindlers arrived in the emperor's city and decided they would take advantage of his fondness for clothes.

The palace guards had orders to admit all weavers and tailors, and the two strangers were soon talking to the emperor.

"We are weavers from a faraway country, where the most wonderful clothes in the world are worn. Our cloth has unbelievably beautiful colours and patterns," they told the emperor, who listened eagerly.

"This very fine cloth," they added slyly, "is invisible to anyone who is stupid or unsuited for his post."

"How useful that would be!" the emperor said to himself. "I'd be able to tell the wise from the foolish, and find out who wasn't fit for his post."

He then ordered his Prime Minister to give the men money, as well as sacks of silk and gold thread so that they could get started.

The two swindlers lost no time. They
rented a big workshop and a loom, and settled
in comfortably. Whenever anyone came by,
they pretended to be hard at work.

Of course, they weren't really weaving at all. They hid a bit of the precious silk and gold thread each day, and spent their time eating and drinking.

"I wonder how those weavers are coming along with their work," the emperor thought. He was a little hesitant about going to see for himself, since the cloth had such magic qualities...not that he need worry!

"I know! I'll send my prime minister!" exclaimed the emperor. "He's not stupid, and he's certainly fit for his post, so the cloth won't be invisible to him."

The emperor summoned the Prime Minister and told him to bring a detailed report of the new cloth.

The news about the weavers who were making the wonderful new cloth had spread throughout the city. The Prime Minister, who was indeed a wise man, decided it would be best to visit the weavers alone.

"Of course, I know I'm fit for my post, and not stupid, but it's best to be on the safe side."

When he arrived, the swindlers were ready for him. Waving their arms grandly, they described the beautiful colours and patterns. One held up cloth that was finished; the other showed him the cloth still on the loom. But the poor Prime Minister couldn't see a thing! "Is it possible that I am really stupid?" he thought.

The Prime Minister returned to the emperor.

"Your majesty," he said solemnly, "I have never seen anything like it." Then he paused, at a loss for words.

"Well? What is it like?" asked the impatient emperor.

"Ah, your majesty...the colours are exquisite, like a beautiful sunset — blue, mauve, pink, and gold. And such intricate patterns — like a garden, with delicate flowers, graceful trees, and rushing streams. I can't believe how clever these weavers are!"

19

After a while, the swindlers asked the Prime Minister for more money. The old man felt that something was wrong, but he was afraid to say that he couldn't see the cloth. He agreed to send them money and more thread the next day.

The next day, the emperor's servants arrived at the workshop, bearing more sacks of gold and silk thread, and a chest filled with gold coins. The swindlers were delighted.

Soon, the emperor grew impatient once more. This time he sent his most fashionable gentleman-in-waiting to see how the weavers were getting along.

The gentleman-in-waiting was shocked to see an empty loom. "Can I be stupid?" he thought. He lifted his eye-glass and pretended to study the cloth.

The gentleman-in-waiting returned to the palace. How could he tell the truth and reveal his stupidity?

And so he, too, praised the beauties of the cloth and described all the wonderful details to the emperor.

$\mathbb{A}$t last, the emperor decided to see the cloth for himself. The swindlers bowed low as they showed him the cloth and described its wonders.

The emperor couldn't believe his eyes. The cloth was invisible to him!

"Here, feel this, your majesty!" said one of the swindlers. "This cloth is as light as a feather."

"Hmm…er…yes, yes — very light. Magnificent stuff, absolutely magnificent," said the emperor.

Soon, the weavers arrived at the palace for a fitting. The emperor stood patiently in his underwear while they pretended to measure and fit the cloth. The courtiers oohed and aahed. "Marvellous!" said one. "Incredible!" cried another. "Your Majesty, you must show the people your new clothes in the procession tomorrow!"

The next day, the swindlers
helped the emperor dress.
Carefully, they handed him
his new clothes, and, just as
carefully, he did his best to
put them on.

"Is everything straight?"
he asked, looking
anxiously at himself
in the mirror.

"Oh, yes,
Your Majesty,"
they exclaimed,
grinning from
ear to ear.

The emperor paraded through the city. All the people cheered and exclaimed how fine the new clothes were, because they were afraid to be thought stupid. Suddenly, a little child cried out, "But he's not wearing any clothes!" Soon, everyone was laughing and saying loudly, "The emperor isn't wearing any clothes!"

The emperor heard them and felt deeply ashamed. "They're right," he thought. Still, he held his head higher than ever, resolving never to mention his true stupidity to anyone. As for the clever swindlers, they disappeared without a trace, taking with them a fortune in gold and fine thread.